Together, they're a PERFECT match!

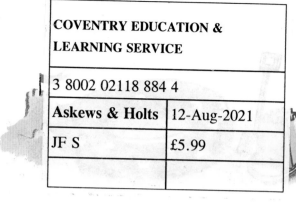

For teachers everywhere!
A special magical "oink!" for all those who
worked in schools during the global pandemic.
Thank you for your dedication.

First published in the UK in 2021 by Usborne Publishing Ltd., Usborne House,
83-85 Saffron Hill, London EC1N 8RT, England, usborne.com

Usborne Verlag, Usborne Publishing Ltd., Prüfeninger Str. 20, 93049 Regensburg,
Deutschland, VK Nr. 17560

Text and illustrations copyright © Hannah Shaw, 2021

This is a work of fiction. The characters, incidents, and dialogues are products of the
author's imagination and are not to be construed as real. Any resemblance to actual events
or persons, living or dead, is entirely coincidental.

A CIP catalogue record for this book is available from the British Library.

ISBN 9781474972192   05662/1   JF AMJJASOND/21

Printed in UAE.

UNIPIGGLE
The Unicorn Pig!

Mermaid
Mayhem

HANNAH SHAW

USBORNE

Twinkleland
Palace & gardens

Hidden
Cove

Better Land

The Harbour

Twinkletown

Bug Island

Village of
Fancy
Pants

Dragonton
Cave
Complex

Volcano
Lake

This is Princess Peony Peachykins Primrose Pollyanna Posh, usually known as Princess Pea. She lives in Twinkleland Palace with her parents, Queen Bee and King Barry.

She likes: mud, marshmallows, chocolate and having fun.

TWINKLELAND!

This is Unipiggle. He's Princess Pea's Royal Companion. He's a loud, muddy and proud unicorn pig.

He likes: mud, marshmallows, chocolate, having fun and getting tickled behind the ears.

Princess Pea was supposed to choose a **UNICORN** as her Royal Companion. But during the Unicorn Parade, there was a **STORM** and things went a bit **WRONG**. Luckily, Unipiggle saved the Princess and the day.

Now Princess Pea and Unipiggle are the best of friends and they love to go on lots of adventures together!

It was lucky the princess didn't choose a real unicorn because they need lots of pampering!

Vegetable Ice Cream

"*Ice cream! Ice cream!*" squeaked a tiny voice.

Princess Pea blinked and looked around. Where had that voice come from?

Unipiggle was snoozing at her feet, and as far as she could see, they were alone on the deck of the Royal Yacht, surrounded by the sparkling sea.

Their Royal Highnesses Queen Bee, King Barry and Princess Pea were on their first ever holiday together. Twinkleland Palace was having a special spring clean, so the Queen and King had decided they would travel to the seaside town of Twee-on-Sea aboard the

The Super Splendid

Royal Yacht, *The Super Splendid*, for some bracing Twinklesea air.

The Royal Yacht lived up to her *Super Splendid* name, with all sorts of ropes to swing from, decks to slide along and cabins to play in.

Princess Pea and Unipiggle had their own cabin with a hammock each and a little porthole they could peer out of. When they'd dropped anchor in Twee-on-Sea Bay, Princess Pea had climbed up to the top deck with her telescope to look for dolphins, admire the little huts along the shore and gaze at the glittery gold beach, which looked perfect for making sandcastles.

Unipiggle hadn't been quite so keen on *The Super Splendid.* As soon as he'd stepped a cautious trotter on board, his legs had gone all **wibbly-wobbly**. Princess Pea had been surprised to see her special piggy companion turn a funny shade of green — from the tip of his magical horn all the way to his curly tail! He really hadn't been his usual happy-go-lucky self since they had left Twinkleland Palace that morning. Now he was lying under the Princess's deck-throne, letting out sad burps.

"Incomiiing!" It was
the squeaky voice again.

Princess Pea looked
up just in time to see
a fairy tumble out
of the sunny sky,
carrying a tray of
ice cream.

"Whooops!" The
fairy landed on his
bottom with a bump
and slid past Princess
Pea along the highly-
polished decking.
Moments later he
reappeared in front of her,

looking sheepish and wearing a cone on his head. "Good afternoon, Your Highness! I'm the Ice-cream Fairy. What would you like to order today?"

Twee-on-Sea Healthy Ices

Garlic & Mushroom
Spinach & Alfalfa
Aubergine & Coriander
Beetroot & Broccoli
Chive & Parsley
Iceberg Lettuce & Cauliflower

All come with cress sprinkles and
a delicious carrot stick.

"Erm…I really can't decide!" Princess Pea gulped. She'd never had an ice cream before, but something told her that they weren't supposed to be quite so *vegetable-y*.

Queen Bee emerged from her cabin and wafted over in her frilly royal holiday outfit. The Ice-cream Fairy presented her with the menu.

"Oh, these look wonderfully wholesome!" gushed the Queen, whose rule on healthy eating was taken very seriously by the subjects of Twinkleland. "How good of you to fly all the way here with Royally Approved treats. I think I'll go for Beetroot & Broccoli flavour, please!"

"I suppose I could try Lettuce & Cauliflower…" Princess Pea mumbled, a little reluctantly. She was going to ask Unipiggle if he wanted one, but he was still snoozing under her throne (or pretending to).

"Did someone mention ice cream?" King Barry asked hopefully, appearing in his snazzy swimwear, twiddling his nautically-styled purple moustache.

He flopped down in his sparkly deck-throne. "I will have the Aubergine & Coriander in a waffle cone, please."

A blob of Princess Pea's lumpy, pale-green ice cream dripped down onto Unipiggle's nose. After a big yawn, the unicorn pig licked it off and rolled out from his hiding place. Princess Pea smiled at him —

he looked much better. She gave him a good scratch behind his ears to cheer him up.

"Ah, I almost forgot to give you your holiday schedule, darling!" The Queen dabbed her mouth with a royal hankie. Princess Pea frowned. She didn't think her mummy understood what "being on holiday" meant.

A Perfect Princess HOLIDAY schedule:

Friday
Count all pebbles on the beach
Holiday-themed spelling test
Shell measuring and sorting
Swimming lesson
Rock-pool tidying
Beach keep-fit session
Quiet time

"Don't worry, I'll be busy too," the Queen said with a big smile. "That beach over there won't rake itself. I can see sand and rocks all

over the place! I'll need to supervise the pixies to get things shipshape."

Princess Pea noticed that King Barry was polishing off his ice cream and keeping quiet about how busy he was intending to be (which was probably not at all).

The King pulled out his mirror to rub some sun cream on his nose.

"Oh, fiddlesticks!"

Unipiggle frowned up at the King, who was now twiddling his moustache and looking very unhappy.

"My moustache! It's **FRIZZY** and **KNOTTY** and there's **ICE CREAM IN IT!**"

Princess Pea winked at Unipiggle. The King spent as much time looking after his moustache

as the Queen did looking after Twinkleland Palace.

"It must be the salty sea breeze! Somebody please fetch my **holiday moustache wax IMMEDIATELY!** This is a moustache emergency!"

A Yacht Pixie scurried off and returned moments later with a large purple tub of gloopy wax.

Unipiggle wrinkled his snout and oinked unhappily. He did *not* like that smell. His cheeks began to turn green again, and his porky legs wobbled this way and that.

Princess Pea was concerned. "Daddy, I think the whiff of your moustache wax is making Unipiggle ill!"

The Princess knew Unipiggle had an excellent sense of smell and could sniff out a nasty whiff

anywhere they went. (Though, handily, he
couldn't smell his own pong.)

"Nonsense, Peasprout! It's such a subtle
aroma and anyway that pig of yours is ten times

pongier than me!" huffed the King. "I must keep up appearances at all times, even on holiday — you never know *who* we'll meet!"

As if on cue, they heard a polite knock on the side of the Royal Yacht.

Knock knock knock.

Princess Pea got up and peered over the handrail.

A group of mermaids and mermen had gathered in the sea below. "Greetings, Princess Pea!" they sang in harmony. "We've come with some very exciting news!"

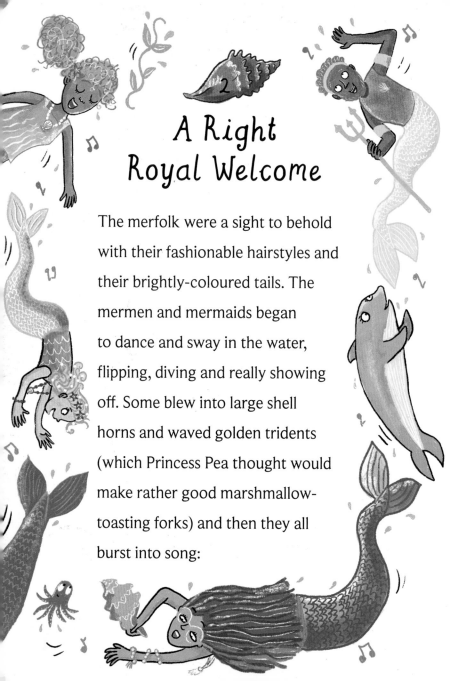

A Right Royal Welcome

The merfolk were a sight to behold with their fashionable hairstyles and their brightly-coloured tails. The mermen and mermaids began to dance and sway in the water, flipping, diving and really showing off. Some blew into large shell horns and waved golden tridents (which Princess Pea thought would make rather good marshmallow-toasting forks) and then they all burst into song:

Oh, Your Majesties!
Hear us sing...
We merfolk come from
Mermaid Springs!
Dive underwater to
see the sights
of coral castles and
plankton lights!
Princess, Piggy,
Queen and King...
Visit the enchanting
Mermaid Springs!

27

Unipiggle oinked excitedly and Princess Pea thought that Mermaid Springs, the underwater town of the merfolk, sounded even *more* fun than visiting the beach at Twee-on-Sea.

"Do they always sing everything?" whispered the King to his daughter.

"Yes, Daddy!" said Princess Pea, who knew a little bit about merfolk because she had read about them in her favourite book, *The Magical Creature Guide*. Her swimming teacher was also a mermaid called Ms Emerald, who gave the Princess lessons in the palace pool.

"Well, hurrah!" The Queen clapped as the merfolk finished their routine. "Although I'm afraid we won't be visiting Mermaid Springs today, as our holiday schedules simply won't allow it!"

Princess Pea did her pouty face, but then smiled when a small porpoise appeared, cleverly balancing a scroll on its nose. Unipiggle blinked. He'd never seen a performing porpoise before!

"My porpoise, Doris, would like you to accept a special invitation!" trilled a familiar mermaid, patting Doris fondly.

It was Ms Emerald!

"Hi, Ms Emerald!" Princess Pea called and her teacher waved back.

A pixie dashed forward, leaned over the side of the yacht and gingerly took the wet scroll from the porpoise. She unrolled it for the King and Queen.

The Merfolk of Mermaid Springs Present:
MUSICAL MOMENTS WITH MERFOLK

We are delighted to host a Special Seaside Concert to welcome and honour the Twinkleland Royal Family.
It will be performed on the beach of Twee-on-Sea, at low tide tonight.

"If you cannot visit Mermaid Springs today," Ms Emerald sang out, "then please do let us give you a Right Royal Welcome at the concert tonight. Everyone in Twee-on-Sea and Mermaid Springs has been invited!"

"This looks **MOST EXCELLENT**," said King Barry immediately.

The Queen was very pleased. "We would love to accept your kind invitation," she said with a big smile.

The group of merfolk bowed so their noses touched the water, then flipped and dived and waved their tails to say farewell.

Princess Pea saw the King reach for his ukulele and she nudged Unipiggle, who let out a concerned little squeal.

"A concert…wonderful, wonderful." The King was always itching to perform with his ukulele, but unfortunately he was terrible at it. His singing had once caused three windows to shatter in Twinkleland Palace and Unipiggle had taken to secretly putting marshmallows in his ears whenever the King started playing.

"Waait…wait a moment!" called the King after the merfolk. "I've just had the most tremendous idea! You see, I'm a bit of a talented musician myself." He stroked his ukulele fondly. "This is the perfect opportunity for you to have a – *ahem* – **royally famous** headline act…

Perhaps I could perform at your concert. What do you think?"

Before the Queen or anyone else could stop him, the King began to play…

The pixies quickly scuttled below deck. Princess Pea took off her flip-flops and held them to her ears, while Unipiggle used half-eaten ice-cream cones as emergency earplugs.

The merfolk looked aghast —
the King's warbling voice and
the twangs from his instrument
were quite simply *unbearable*.

As the song droned on,
the sea started to churn.

"That's quite **ENOUGH**,
Barry!" The Queen shushed him
as waves began to rock the yacht.

But the King wouldn't listen.
He was just reaching a painful
crescendo when...

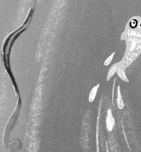

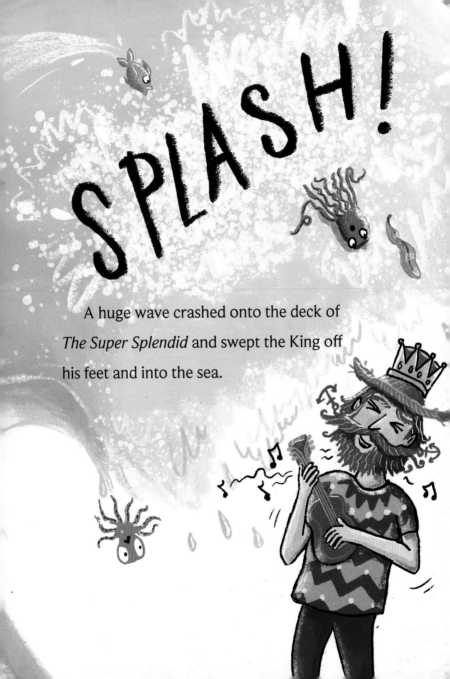

SPLASH!

A huge wave crashed onto the deck of *The Super Splendid* and swept the King off his feet and into the sea.

The Queen shrieked and grasped the handrail. Princess Pea and Unipiggle watched in horror as the King was sucked **down**, **down**, down into a swirling whirlpool. And then he vanished!

Mermaid Mayhem

All was strangely silent as the sea calmed. The merfolk, their ears still ringing from the King's dreadful performance, looked baffled, and the Queen was opening and shutting her mouth but no sound was coming out.

Unipiggle broke the hush with an astounded "OINK!"

Then… Princess Pea gasped, the merfolk all started talking at once, Doris the Porpoise squeaked and flapped her flippers and the Yacht Pixies peered out of their portholes and wailed woefully together. It was **MAYHEM!**

The King is gooone!

"Oh dear! He'll not survive for long down there! And what about his poor moustache?" cried the Queen.

A merman with shells in his beard blew into his trumpet and everyone stopped what they were doing and looked at him.

"Your Majesty, I'm Shellbeard. Please fear not — the King will be able to breathe underwater. You see, the ancient magic of Twinklesea means

TOOT!

that anyone is able to breathe down there as if they were on land," he explained.

This was news to Queen Bee and Princess Pea!

The Queen looked relieved, but she also had some questions. "How can the King have just **disappeared** like that? Where has he gone? Was any **other** magic used?" The Queen narrowed her eyes suspiciously at Unipiggle. Using magic was strictly forbidden in Twinkleland because it was messy and unpredictable. (Unipiggle often ignored this, however, and used his magical horn to turn things into chocolate.)

"Unipiggle had nothing to do with this!" protested Princess Pea. Unipiggle snorted indignantly.

Shellbeard sang out again: "We merfolk may know where the King has gone…"

"Please come aboard and **EXPLAIN** everything!" demanded Queen Bee.

"Ms Emerald should join us too!" Princess Pea said quickly, beckoning to her teacher.

Shellbeard and Ms Emerald were soon sitting awkwardly on the deck in a shallow paddling pool that the Yacht Pixies had filled with water. Unipiggle had wanted to join them but there wasn't any room for him.

For once Shellbeard didn't sing — instead he lowered his voice, leaned forward and whispered dramatically, "Mermaid Springs is a wonderful place, but there is something…**someone**…that **LURKS** nearby! Some say it is an ancient magical creature; we merfolk call it **THE BELCHER** — but no one has ever set eyes on it! We believe it sleeps most of the time, but occasionally it belches so loudly that it blows the roof tiles off our coral homes and causes giant waves to wash right up to the beach huts in Twee-on-Sea. Perhaps the King's performance woke **THE BELCHER**?"

Unipiggle grunted but Princess Pea couldn't help a little smile; even if she was worried about her daddy, a burping magical sea creature sounded rather funny to her.

Ms Emerald looked serious. "It makes magical whirlpools and sucks anything it wants into them. Only four tides ago a mermaid was playing her recorder on the rocks and her instrument was sucked away!

THE BELCHER must have the King! But there's a problem; we've no idea where the creature lurks. No one has ever tried to find out, as we merfolk are too afraid to disturb it!"

The Queen folded her arms. "Firstly, I'm not best pleased there is a magical creature I haven't heard of in my own kingdom… Secondly, if this **BELCHER** exists, it must be found immediately. The King must be rescued!"

Ms Emerald and Shellbeard looked at each other miserably. They didn't know what to do.

Princess Pea thought hard. There had to be a way to find her daddy.

Then…

SQUELCH!

OH, YUCK!

The Princess had accidentally put her foot into the King's tub of **holiday moustache wax**.

Unipiggle stuck out his tongue and wrinkled his nose in disgust.

"I've got it!" cried Princess Pea all of a sudden, wiping the moustache wax off her flip-flop. "I know how to find King Barry!"

A Pongy Plan

Princess Pea and Unipiggle were nearly ready for their rescue mission!

"All set for an undersea adventure, Unipiggle?" the Princess called as she pulled on her flippers and found a waterproof torch in her cabin (just in case).

Unipiggle oinked loudly. He was wearing an inflatable rubber ring and a snorkel and had eaten a marshmallow (just in case).

But the Queen didn't seem convinced by her daughter's plan. "Let me get this straight – you think Unipiggle will be able to sniff out poor Barry underwater?"

"He will!" Princess Pea grinned. "You see, Daddy's moustache wax is no ordinary wax. It is super-waterproof and has a **VERY strong pong**! Unipiggle should be able to follow the scent from miles away. If what the merfolk say is true, we'll find where this **BELCHER** creature is hiding, and then rescue Daddy when **THE BELCHER** is asleep!"

"Oink! Oink!" Unipiggle nodded enthusiastically, although Princess Pea felt a bit sorry that he would keep having to **SNIFF THE WHIFF**!

"Very well. I suppose we don't have any other choice," the Queen agreed reluctantly. "But you can't go alone!"

"As Princess Pea's swimming teacher, I think I should guide her on this important mission," volunteered Ms Emerald bravely.

Shellbeard looked relieved that Ms Emerald had offered first. "And I shall swim down to Mermaid Springs while you get ready, to inform the other merfolk of the plan," the merman declared quickly. He dived off the side of the yacht and vanished in a trail of bubbles.

"I will wait here and keep watch in case Barry re-emerges. The beach tidy-up will have to wait!" The Queen sighed, scanning the horizon for any sign of the missing King.

"One... Two... Three..."

SPLOOSH!

Princess Pea leaped into the sea and Ms Emerald executed a perfect backwards dive with a twist and two-and-a-half somersaults.

Unipiggle managed to do an extra-big belly flop. He had taken great care to apply a nice thick layer of mud sunscreen that morning and now a sticky brown puddle floated on the surface of the water around him.

There was a whistle and a squeak and Doris the Porpoise popped up beside them in the water, squeaking and clapping her flippers excitedly.

Doris says she wants to help us too.

Porpoise speech sounded very squeaky to Princess Pea, and she was pleased Ms Emerald could translate what Doris was saying!

"Do take care," called out the Queen, waving goodbye from her deck-throne. "And it would be very convenient if you *could* bring the King back before the concert tonight. We don't want to miss our **Right Royal Welcome**!"

Princess Pea and Unipiggle dived down,
following Ms Emerald's shimmering tail into
the blue. The Princess was delighted to find
that as well as being able to breathe underwater,
she could speak and hear easily too.

Doris demonstrated how to do an
underwater roly-poly and Unipiggle was
very amused to find that he could blow large
balloon-like bubbles from both his mouth and
his bottom! He darted around, joyfully popping
them with his magical horn.

Ms Emerald pointed out the town of Mermaid Springs in a sandy valley on the seabed. Pink coral castles with turrets to rival Twinkleland Palace rose out of the depths and the whole place sparkled enticingly.

"Welcome to my home," Ms Emerald sang proudly. "Not many Twinkleland folk have been here. Everyone always visits Twee-on-Sea instead and forgets about our little haven beneath the waves."

"Well, I can't wait to see more," said Princess Pea, trying out a roly-poly. She held on tight to Unipiggle's horn and together they swam into Mermaid Springs.

Marvellous
Mermaid Springs

Princess Pea's flippers touched down on the
sandy main street of Mermaid Springs and she
gazed around at the sights. Unipiggle swam
around her and immediately started trying to
SNIFF THE WHIFF.

"Why is everything **glowing**?" Princess Pea
asked in awe.

"The lights are kindly provided by our
luminous plankton friends," explained
Ms Emerald. "Aren't they **dazzling**?"

SHELL SHOP

They swam through the glittery undersea town. Princess Pea could see that the swirls and stars that decorated the buildings around them were actually sea snails and starfish. But something wasn't quite right…

Except for a few darting fish and curious crabs, the streets were eerily empty.

"Mermaid Springs seems very quiet," Princess Pea thought out loud. "Where's Shellbeard gone?"

"He was very worried about us disturbing **THE BELCHER**. I think he must have warned the other merfolk to stay inside!" sang Ms Emerald.

"Oh." Princess Pea gulped, suddenly feeling very uneasy about what might lie ahead.

Doris put a comforting flipper on Princess Pea's shoulder and Ms Emerald smiled, although she also looked a little nervous. "I'm sure it will all work out — we're both here to help you and Unipiggle rescue the King, and I think we make a great team!"

Princess Pea grinned. "Okay, Royal Rescue Team! Where do we start looking?"

Unipiggle was already on the case — he'd obviously **SNIFFED THE WHIFF** because he swam off with an eager oink. Princess Pea, Ms Emerald and Doris followed him over rolling underwater sand dunes and rock gardens.

As they drifted through the beautiful seascape, it was hard not to be distracted by all the underwater rainbows, an interesting shipwreck full of unclaimed treasure, and what turned out to be very bouncy rocks.

"Mermaid Springs is so much **FUN!**"
laughed Princess Pea, bouncing right over
Doris the Porpoise.

"Try a wild sea-berry." Ms Emerald paused
to pick a handful of ripe berries. Unipiggle
swallowed them in one go.

Princess Pea licked her lips and popped
a few in her mouth. "Mmm, they taste a bit
like marshmallows!"

A strawberry jelly
floated past. Doris
the Porpoise
squeaked in
horror as
Unipiggle eyed
it hungrily.

"Oh no! Don't eat it!" Ms Emerald warned him. "That's a jelly*fish*, not a jelly!"

Princess Pea's tummy did a little tumble as she suddenly had the awful thought that her daddy could make a tasty snack for a **MONSTROUS** belching sea-creature! She'd been having so much fun that she'd almost forgotten they were supposed to be on an important rescue mission.

Princess Pea quickly gave her piggy companion an encouraging tickle. "Hurry now, Unipiggle. Show us where to go next!"

Unipiggle immediately started sniffing again, sampling all the underwater currents around them. As a particularly wavy one whooshed past, he snorted and pulled a yucky face.

"Poor piggy!" cried Princess Pea. "Be brave! The pong is guiding us!" She beckoned to the others. "This way to the King!"

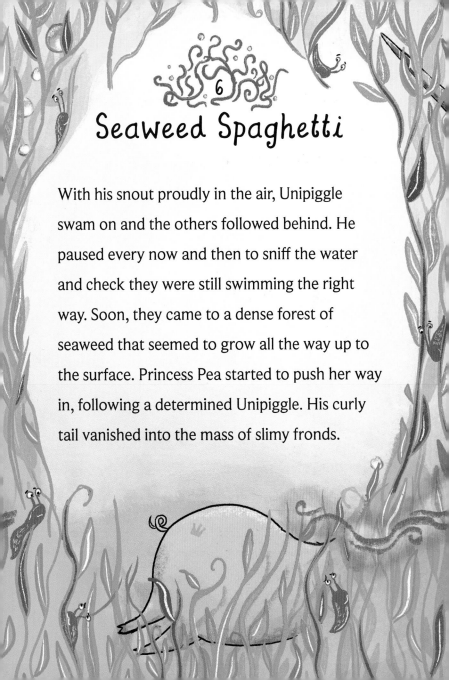

6
Seaweed Spaghetti

With his snout proudly in the air, Unipiggle swam on and the others followed behind. He paused every now and then to sniff the water and check they were still swimming the right way. Soon, they came to a dense forest of seaweed that seemed to grow all the way up to the surface. Princess Pea started to push her way in, following a determined Unipiggle. His curly tail vanished into the mass of slimy fronds.

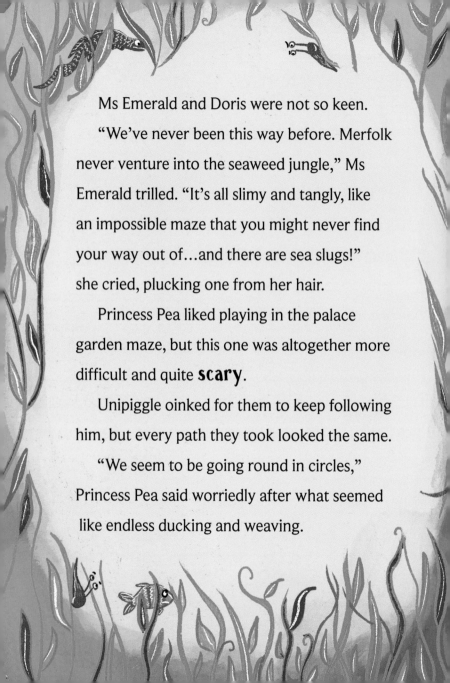

Ms Emerald and Doris were not so keen.

"We've never been this way before. Merfolk never venture into the seaweed jungle," Ms Emerald trilled. "It's all slimy and tangly, like an impossible maze that you might never find your way out of…and there are sea slugs!" she cried, plucking one from her hair.

Princess Pea liked playing in the palace garden maze, but this one was altogether more difficult and quite **scary**.

Unipiggle oinked for them to keep following him, but every path they took looked the same.

"We seem to be going round in circles," Princess Pea said worriedly after what seemed like endless ducking and weaving.

"What if we are lost in here for ever!" She flopped down on a little rock. "Whoops!" The rock she sat on started to move…and Princess Pea fell backwards through a thick wall of kelp. "I'm sorry, I thought you were a rock!" she apologized to a disgruntled sea turtle as it swam away.

But as she stood up, Princess Pea found herself in a clearing. There ahead, almost hidden by a curtain of seaweed, she caught a glimpse of what looked like an entrance to a cave. She swam a little closer… From deep within she could hear a distinct sound: **Twang! Strum! Strum!**

Princess Pea's heart started thumping. It was a ukulele! Could it be the King? Was **THE BELCHER** making him play? Or perhaps the King was fighting **THE BELCHER** with his only weapon: his ear-bending music!

There was something not quite right…
Had the King's playing magically improved?
Princess Pea wondered. It sounded so tuneful.

Her thoughts were interrupted when Unipiggle, Ms Emerald and Doris stuck their heads through the wall of kelp. "Come through, quick!" hissed Princess Pea, beckoning for them to join her.

"That must be **THE BELCHER**'s Lair!" Ms Emerald gasped. Doris the Porpoise shuddered.

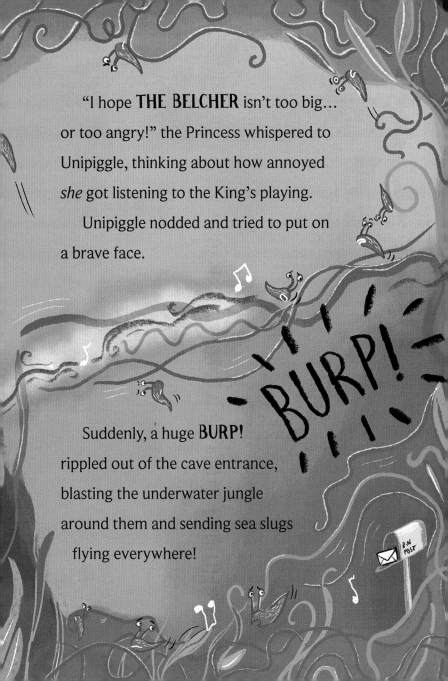

"I hope **THE BELCHER** isn't too big… or too angry!" the Princess whispered to Unipiggle, thinking about how annoyed *she* got listening to the King's playing.

Unipiggle nodded and tried to put on a brave face.

Suddenly, a huge **BURP!** rippled out of the cave entrance, blasting the underwater jungle around them and sending sea slugs flying everywhere!

BURP!

"This is definitely the right place!" declared Princess Pea. Unipiggle wiggled his tail and they got ready to investigate…

BUT the force of the burp had dislodged an enormous tumbleweed tangle of sticky seaweed, and it was rolling straight towards them!

"SWIM!" yelled Princess Pea.

But it was too late! The seaweed was upon them.

Unipiggle got twisted and tangled as he tried to escape. Princess Pea found herself all tied up in knots, while Doris the Porpoise and Ms Emerald wiggled and writhed but only got more tightly stuck. It was no use. The Royal Rescue Team were well and truly **trapped**!

"How can we get to the King now?" cried Princess Pea. Unipiggle oinked sorrowfully — he couldn't even move his head to use his magic horn.

The sound of ukulele music reached their ears once more, followed by a distant rumbling noise.

"Is that **THE BELCHER**... snoring?" wondered Princess Pea.

It was an important part of the plan that
THE BELCHER stayed asleep.

"I do hope so," Ms Emerald sang. "If only we weren't trapped in this sea spaghetti, now would be the right time to attempt our mission!"

"What did you say this type of seaweed is called?" Princess Pea asked curiously.

"Why, sea spaghetti of course," Ms Emerald warbled. "It's perfectly edible, and somewhat delicious…"

If there was one thing Princess Pea and Unipiggle knew how to do, it was eat delicious food! Unipiggle had once saved Princess Pea from a pile of giant marshmallows by eating them all, and it looked like his heroic gobbling was about to come in handy again…

Unipiggle and the Princess started chewing at the tangles, gobbling and slurping up as much of the sea spaghetti as they could.

> NOM nom! Gobble! Gobble! SLURP!

It wasn't long before the giant ball of seaweed started to unravel as the rescuers munched themselves free. "That was yummy!" Princess Pea said.

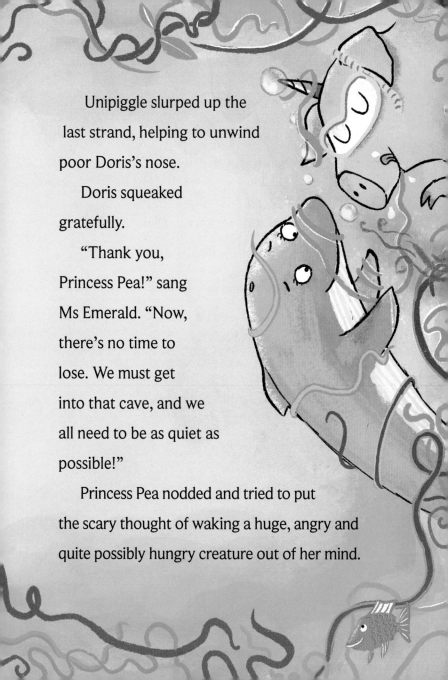

Unipiggle slurped up the last strand, helping to unwind poor Doris's nose.

Doris squeaked gratefully.

"Thank you, Princess Pea!" sang Ms Emerald. "Now, there's no time to lose. We must get into that cave, and we all need to be as quiet as possible!"

Princess Pea nodded and tried to put the scary thought of waking a huge, angry and quite possibly hungry creature out of her mind.

She switched on her waterproof torch and gave it to Unipiggle. The brave unicorn pig entered the cave first, sniffing all the while. The others followed, swimming cautiously through dark passages lined with ancient, peeling wallpaper and murky paintings, as the sounds of snoring and the twanging of strings got louder.

Unipiggle stopped and signalled to the others. The **moustache-wax pong** was very strong here! The King was close by...but that meant the dreaded **BELCHER** might be too.

Ms Emerald put her finger to her lips as the passage widened into a larger cavern.

Princess Pea gave Ms Emerald a thumbs up, but Unipiggle was looking rather uncomfortable — his tummy was too full of sea spaghetti.
He frowned as it churned noisily.

Then…

PARRRRRP!

A very large, stinky bubble escaped from Unipiggle's bottom. Princess Pea, Ms Emerald and Doris dived out of the way to avoid it. The ukulele playing stopped.

"HELLLLO? IS SOMEONE THEREEEEE?" boomed a deep voice that certainly didn't belong to the King.

"Yikes!" gasped Princess Pea. "We've been rumbled!"

The Belcher

Princess Pea, Unipiggle, Ms Emerald and Doris held their breath as they waited to hear what **THE BELCHER** would say next. But then…

WHOOSH!

A swirling whirlpool of water sucked the rescuers further into **THE BELCHER**'s cave.

When the water stopped churning around them, they could see that they were in a vast, brightly-lit cavern, aglow with plankton lights.

And in the centre of the cave, upon a large, ornate coral sofa sat an **ENORMOUS WHALE.**

It was **THE BELCHER**! And he was **so BIG**! Princess Pea felt very alarmed.

Until brave Unipiggle swam forwards and gave a happy oink.

The whale had a long pointy rainbow horn, just like Unipiggle's!

Even more surprisingly, he was strumming King Barry's ukulele! The ukulele looked tiny in the whale's flippers, but he was playing it much better than the King could.

A loud ZZZZZZZZ sound escaped from the corner of the room and the Princess was surprised to see her daddy was fast asleep and snoring! She felt very relieved. He didn't look like he needed rescuing at all!

"Welcome! I wasn't expecting more guests!" boomed the whale.

Ms Emerald was amazed. "You're a narwhal," she warbled.

Doris the Porpoise peeped out from where she'd hidden herself behind Ms Emerald and squeaked a porpoisey "Hello!"

The narwhal smiled warmly. "I am a narwhal," he said shyly, "but I'm no ordinary narwhal. I'm **BURPEE**, the last of the **giant magical narwhals**. I'm astonished you're here — no one has ever found my cave as it's so well hidden!"

His eyes rested on
Unipiggle, who
proudly stuck his
snout in the air.
"A unicorn
pig?" Burpee
chuckled.
"I thought *I*
was rare!"
"So it
is you who
makes the
whirlpools
in Mermaid
Springs?"
Princess Pea asked.

"Oh yes, sometimes this old magic tusk comes in useful for getting the things I want without leaving my cave," mused the narwhal.

"But what are you doing with my daddy?" demanded the Princess, pointing to the King.

"Oh... That was a bit of a mistake!" admitted Burpee. "I only wanted to borrow his instrument. I heard him playing and thought I might like to have a go myself. As you can see, I have borrowed quite a few music-making devices over the years."

Princess Pea and Unipiggle looked around
and noticed the many musical instruments
displayed on the walls of the cave.

Ms Emerald examined the narwhal's
collection. "I do believe some of these belonged
to my friends," she sang, with a raised eyebrow.

"Oh dear, really?" Burpee turned back to the Princess, hastily changing the subject. "Anyway, your daddy told me he was the **King of Twinkleland**! I wasn't sure whether to believe him or not but we did have a good old chat about music and whether having a moustache or a tusk was better. I was about to return him to the surface, but after a cup of shrimp tea and some rock cakes, he dozed off." The narwhal began to absent-mindedly strum the ukulele again, a big whaley smile on his face.

"You're very good at playing the ukulele," Princess Pea said.

"*Oink!*" agreed Unipiggle.

Ms Emerald looked impressed too. "You do

play beautifully. You should perform at our concert tonight!" she suggested.

"Well, thank you!" Burpee blushed a bright shade of pink. "But I couldn't possibly… I'm too shy! I never normally have an audience, you see. I'm quite happy hiding out here on my own, jamming and eating sea spaghetti."

"Is that what makes you so…burpy?" asked Princess Pea, giggling and letting out a small burp of bubbles herself. The narwhal blushed again. "Oh, I'm **SUCH** a windy whale!" he complained. "My diet of sea spaghetti and shrimp tea plays havoc with my digestion."

Unipiggle gave Princess Pea a nudge. It was time to head back. The Queen would be very worried by now.

"Well, we are sorry to disturb you, Mr Burpee, sir, but please could you give us a helping whirl back to the surface? We don't want to miss the concert or worry my mummy the Queen any further." She looked over at the snoring King. "There's no need to wake Daddy before you send us up!"

Burpee's tusk started glowing.

Until next time, new friends!

Princess Pea grabbed hold of Unipiggle and the King as she felt the water swirling around them again, and a burst of bubbles tickled their toes as they were blasted gently up towards the surface. Ms Emerald and Doris sang farewell and dived down to Mermaid Springs to spread the good news that everyone was safe and sound.

"What? What!?" the King gargled suddenly, spluttering awake as they emerged from the waves.

Princess Pea and Unipiggle could see the Queen on the deck of *The Super Splendid* and waved as much as they could. They'd had such an adventure, but it was nice to be back.

"My darling Peony Peachykins Primrose! And Barry! You're back!" cried the Queen as she spotted them. "Thank goodness! It's almost low tide — time for the concert," she said.

As Princess Pea, Unipiggle and the King clambered onto *The Super Splendid*, the Queen gave the King a quick peck on the nose and Princess Pea a squeeze. Then she jumped into a waiting dinghy and pointed towards the shore.

"That beach is not fit for a Royal Concert. Those Twee-on-Sea folk need my help! I've been looking at those unpolished rocks, sandy crevices and weedy dunes all afternoon. I must get started with my Raking Pixies to set everything straight for the concert! There's no time to lose. Toodle pip!"

-little Splendid-

8

Concert on the Rocks

The King, the Princess and Unipiggle were all feeling a little soggy after their undersea escapades. But the Yacht Pixies quickly brought them dry robes, then pounced on Unipiggle and wrapped him up in a towel. Princess Pea thought he looked like a sausage roll!

Two Hair Pixies were summoned and they both started trying to tame the King's moustache with combs and a hairdryer.

"I had a funny dream," the King told Princess Pea, still looking slightly dazed. "I dreamed I was in an undersea cavern with an enormous magical talking whale, who was very interested in playing my ukulele…" The King stopped and looked around him. "Oh! My ukulele!" he wailed. "I must have lost it when I fell into the water!"

"Oops!" said Princess Pea, catching Unipiggle's eye.

Unipiggle gave her an enormous wink. Of course, they knew exactly where it was; they'd let Burpee keep it.

"It's a good thing I have a spare ukulele back at the palace," the King continued. "But what am I going to do at the concert tonight? I promised the merfolk I'd be the headline act!" He sighed and threw his arms into the air dramatically. "I suppose they'll just have to cancel the whole thing…" He waved his hands around. "I was looking forward to it so much!" He flung his arms out wide, accidentally knocking a comb from a pixie's grasp.

"I don't think Mummy or the merfolk will want to cancel the concert," Princess Pea reassured him. "You'll still be a special royal guest in the audience."

This didn't really cheer up the King, whose dreams had been dashed, and his arms slumped to his sides.

"Unless..." the Princess said, her eyes lighting up. "Daddy, put your arms in the air again? Flap your hands around? That's it! I've just had a brilliant idea!"

At sunset, the King stepped up onto the beautiful Twee-on-Sea stage to polite clapping from the audience, who were sitting on the Queen's freshly raked, polished and reorganized beach. Princess Pea waved at her daddy, but the King was too busy straightening his bow tie on his super-smart tuxedo and checking his moustache even though it was curled and waxed to perfection.

Shellbeard blew a long and melodious *Toooot!* from his shell trumpet.

TOOOOT!

"This is our special
Royal Concert and
we're lucky to have
King Barry here…er…
helping us to perform,"
he chanted.

The King thanked him
and spoke to the crowd of loyal,
royal fans. "Ladies and gentle merfolk, boys,
girls, pixies, Unipigs, porpoises and…er…fish.

Earlier today, tragedy struck when my ukulele vanished into the dark heart of the ocean…"
He wiped a tear from his eye; Princess Pea and Unipiggle giggled. Ms Emerald and Shellbeard and all the other merfolk nodded along sympathetically as the King began his sorry tale, but the Queen folded her arms.

"Do cut to the point, Barry," she called out.

"Alas, I was going to give up on the whole concert, but my heroic daughter Peasprout and

her wonderful Unipiggle suggested a superb, alternative starring role for me." The King grasped his gold moustache comb, raised both arms in the air and started waving his hands around.

"*Laaaaaaaaaa!*" sang the merfolk and the concert began.

"I didn't know Barry could conduct," whispered the surprised Queen to her daughter over the soothing sound of merfolk harmony.

"I'm not sure he can, Mummy!" replied Princess Pea with a giggle.

"Well, at least he's quiet," said the Queen with a satisfied smile.

And Princess Pea and Unipiggle smiled too. Everything had worked out just as they had planned!

A Whale of a Time

The twinkling stars came out as the merfolk played their final song. Princess Pea and Unipiggle had sneaked away to make sandcastles. Unipiggle had even dug a great big hole to wallow in.

"That was hard work!" said the King, coming over still waving his comb and wafting whiffs of

moustache wax over everyone.

"How about another healthy ice cream?" announced the Queen generously.

Unipiggle trotted off to find the Ice-cream Fairy. He returned with a cheeky glint in his eye and his horn aglow, balancing a tray of ice creams on his back.

"Oh look, it appears there's only chocolate flavour left!" Princess Pea pointed out with glee.

Ms Emerald and Doris the Porpoise called to Princess Pea from the water. "Would Your Highness like to go for a moonlit swim?"

"Please may I?" Princess Pea begged the Queen.

The Queen was rather engrossed by her chocolate ice cream — even though she had made it clear that she didn't approve of it, for some reason she couldn't stop eating it. "Very well, but come back soon for bedtime and beware of those whirlpools!"

Princess Pea and Unipiggle ran down the beach and jumped into the waves.

1...2...3... SPLASH!

As they floated around under the stars in Unipiggle's rubber ring, the mermaids and mermen of Twinklesea sent them a gift of glowing plankton to light up the sea around them.

"I love holiday adventures," Princess Pea sighed happily.

Then, from somewhere not too far away, they heard a **jiggly** beat, a **jiving** rhythm and a **funky** ukulele tune. Their narwhal friend BURPEE was playing music just for them.

Princess Pea laughed and Unipiggle oinked joyfully, and they danced in the surf until they could dance no more.

HOW TO DRAW A NARWHAL

You will need: a pencil, a black pen, a rubber and colouring pencils.

Step 1: Use a pencil to draw one teardrop shape and one triangle like this...

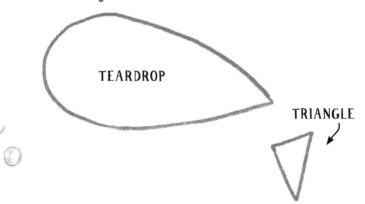

TEARDROP

TRIANGLE

Step 2: Add shapes for the horn, eye, flippers and tail.

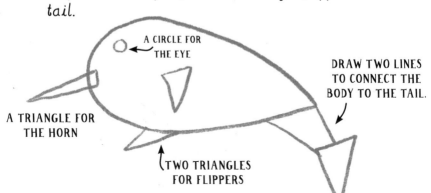

A CIRCLE FOR THE EYE

DRAW TWO LINES TO CONNECT THE BODY TO THE TAIL.

A TRIANGLE FOR THE HORN

TWO TRIANGLES FOR FLIPPERS

Step 3: Use a pen to draw your narwhal on top of the pencil shapes.

COPY THIS FACE...

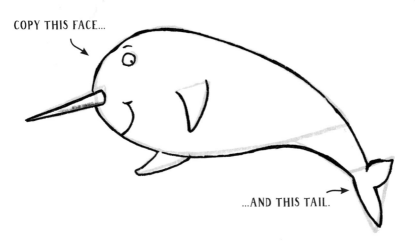

...AND THIS TAIL.

Step 4: Wait for the ink to dry, then rub out all of the pencil lines. Now it's time to colour in your narwhal, using your colouring pencils!

REMEMBER TO GIVE YOUR NARWHAL A NAME, TOO!

SPOT THE DIFFERENCE

Can you find EIGHT differences between these two pictures?

Keep a list of the differences you spot.

Turn the page for a Unipiggle quiz and the answers...

A LOUD, MUDDY
and PROUD UNIPIGGLE quiz!

1) What is the Royal Yacht called?

2) Can you name one of the ice-cream flavours that the Ice-cream Fairy offers Princess Pea and Unipiggle?

3) Which instrument does the King play?

4) Where do the merfolk live?

5) What does Unipiggle follow to help him find the King?

6) Which sort of animal is Doris?

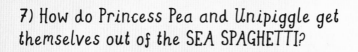

7) How do Princess Pea and Unipiggle get themselves out of the SEA SPAGHETTI?

8) What *is* THE BELCHER's real name?

9) Look back at p90-91. How many musical instruments can you count on the wall of the cave?

10) What do THE BELCHER and Unipiggle have in common?

11) Which flavour does Unipiggle transform the ice cream into at the end?

ANSWERS

QUIZ

1) The Royal Yacht is called "The Super Splendid".

2) The ice-cream flavours are: Garlic & Mushroom; Spinach & Alfalfa; Aubergine & Coriander; Beetroot & Broccoli; Chive & Parsley; Iceberg Lettuce & Cauliflower. All come with cress sprinkles and a delicious carrot stick.

3) The King plays a ukulele.

4) The merfolk live in Mermaid Springs.

5) Unipiggle follows the smell of the King's moustache wax to find him (he SNIFFS the WHIFF!).

6) Doris is a porpoise.

7) Princess Pea and Unipiggle eat (rather slurpily) the sea spaghetti! Yum!

8) The Belcher's name is Burpee.

9) There are 11 musical instruments on the wall.

10) The Belcher and Unipiggle both have rainbow-coloured horns.

11) Unipiggle turns the ice creams into chocolate ice creams at the end.

SPOT THE DIFFERENCE

For more UNIPIGGLE activities, trot to:
www.unipiggle.com

UNIPIGGLE
The Unicorn Pig!

Collect more adventures from UNIPIGGLE
and PRINCESS PEA...

Meet the princess who loves breaking the rules,
and her Royal Unicorn who happens to be a pig!

It's the day of the Royal Unicorn
Parade, and Princess Pea has
to choose her own perfect
UNICORN. But then Unipiggle
appears and creates a very big
MUDDLE!